Kes Gray

Mom
and
Dad
Glue

Illustrated by

Lee Wildish

BARRON'S

My mom and dad are broken,
I don't know what to do.

My mom and dad have come undone,
I need to find some glue.

I need a pot of parent glue
To stick them back together.

I need to patch their marriage up,
I need to make them better.

I need to stick their smiles back on,
I need to get them mended.

I need them to be mom and dad,
The way they were intended.

They used to kiss
and cuddle,
But now they tut
and sigh.

They're breaking up.
    They're breaking up.

Am
I
the
reason
why?

They both say don't be silly,
That no one is to blame.

Although it's not worked out for them,
They love me just the same.

My friends say not to worry,
My friends say I'll be fine.

Lots of parents separate,

But
no,
no,
no!
Not
mine!

I need a pot of parent glue,
I need to find some fast.

I need to make them whole again,
I need to make them last.

I'm standing in the glue shop,
As far as I can see.

There's every glue that you could want,
Unless that you is me.

There's glue for model airplanes,

There's glue for plates and drawers.

There's glue for paper, glue for wood,

There's glue for tiles and floors.

There's super fast and super strong,

There's tubes and pots and tins.

Where every row of wrong glue starts,
Another one begins.

The owner of the glue shop
Asks what my glue is for.

And when she hears my answer
She softly shuts the door.

She puts her arm around me
And says it's time to see.

That sometimes life works out this way,
That what must be must be.

I need to look beyond the break,
I need to think ahead.

I need to see that families
Can live apart instead.

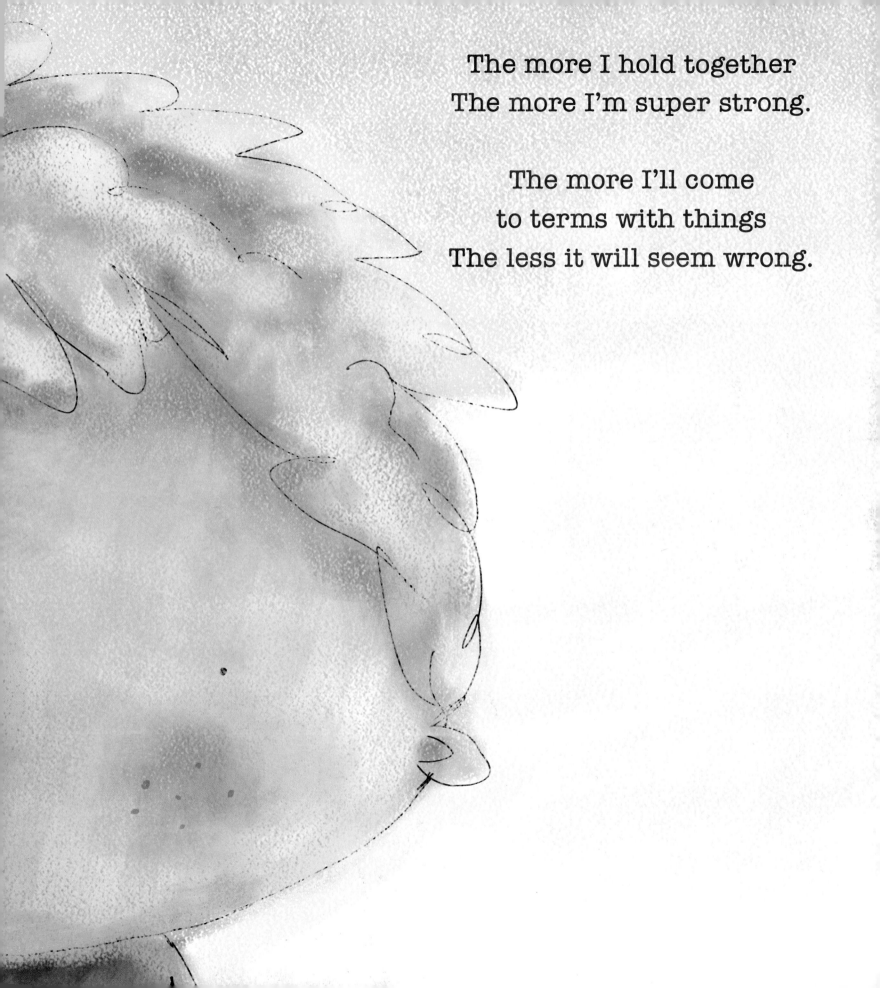

The more I hold together
The more I'm super strong.

The more I'll come
to terms with things
The less it will seem wrong.

But there's one thing
to remember,
And this should
mean a lot.

My parents may
be broken,
But their love for
me is not.

Their love for me will never break,
It's chip and shatter free.

It also comes with something else,
A life-time guarantee.

We will love you forever
We will love you forever
We will love you forever
We will love you forever
We will love you forever

I thank her for her kindness
And turn toward the door.

I wave to the adhesives
And leave with so much more.

If mom and dad could mend themselves
They would have done by now.

The will, the should, the must is there.
What's missing is the how.

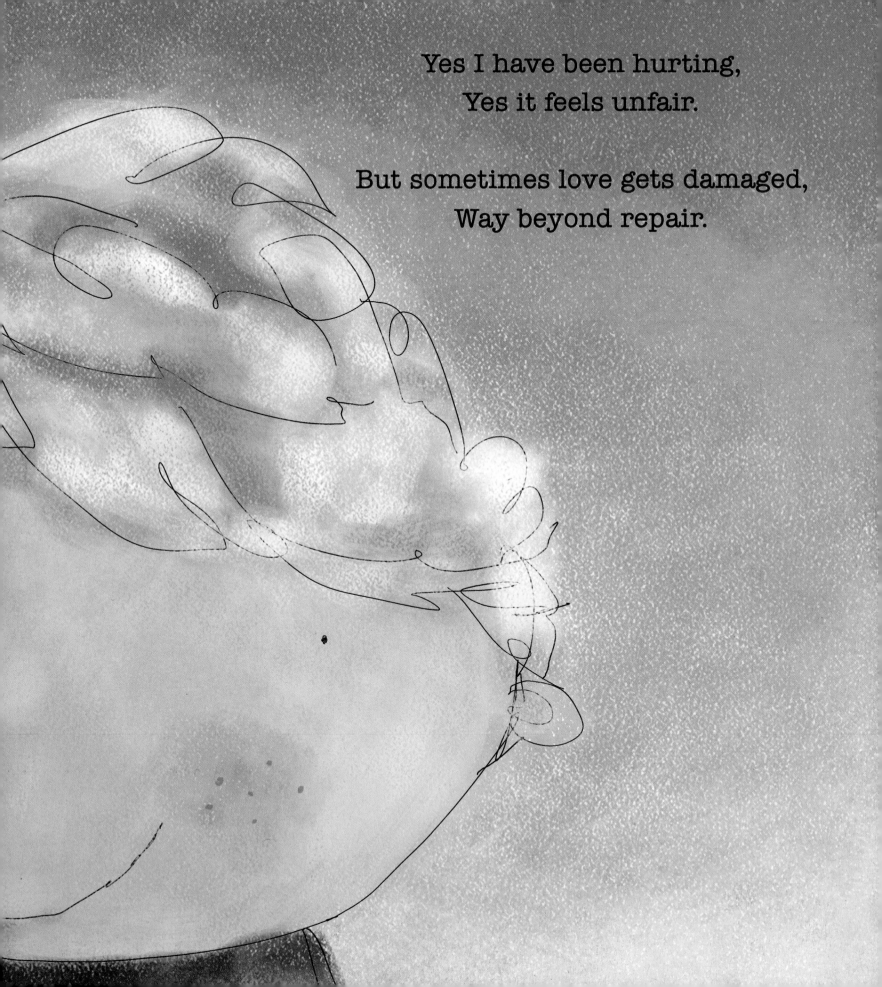

Yes I have been hurting,
Yes it feels unfair.

But sometimes love gets damaged,
Way beyond repair.

I pull my life together
And smile as I depart.

I need to make the best of things,
There is no glue for hearts.

To everyone at Gingerbread K.G.

First edition for the United States published
in 2009 by Barron's Educational Series, Inc.

First published in hardback 2009 by Hodder Children's Books,
338 Euston Road, London, England NW1 3BH

Text copyright © Kes Gray 2009
Illustration © Lee Wildish 2009

All inquiries should be addressed to:
Barron's Educational Series, Inc.
250 Wireless Boulevard
Hauppauge, New York 11788
www.barronseduc.com

ISBN-13: 978-0-7641-6262-6
ISBN-10: 0-7641-6262-4

Library of Congress Control No. 2009922387

Printed and bound in China

9 8 7 6 5 4 3 2 1